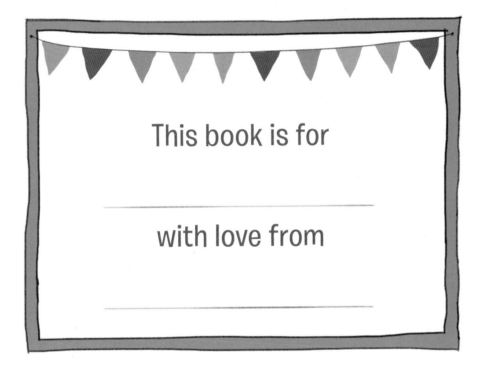

This book is for

_____

with love from

_____

WiTH Dad, IT'S LiKe THaT

Nadine Brun-Cosme

Pictures by Magali Le Huche

Albert Whitman & Company
Chicago, Illinois

For Simon—NBC

For Clara and Thomas—MLH

Library of Congress Cataloging-in-Publication
data is on file with the publisher.

Copyright © Flammarion
Text by Nadine Brun-Cosme
Pictures by Magali Le Huche
First published in 2012 in France by Flammarion as *Avec Moi Cést Comme Ça*
Published in 2016 by Albert Whitman & Company
ISBN 978-0-8075-8731-7

Printed in China
10 9 8 7 6 5 4 3 2 1 LP 24 23 22 21 20 19 18 17 16 15

For more information about Albert Whitman & Company,
visit our web site at www.albertwhitman.com.

Mom is at the movies.

That means that, tonight, Dad is in charge.

"Bath time is first, Clare!" Dad announces.

But when Clare hops in, the bathwater is a little too cold. And her favorite toy crocodile gets lost at the bottom of the tub.

"Dad," says Clare, "that's not how Mom does it. With Mom, the temperature is always just right. And she makes Crocodile nibble my toes."

"Ah!" says Dad. "Just your toes? I think Crocodile wants to gobble up this entire girl!"

Crocodile pounces on Clare's feet, her belly, and her nose, and Clare laughs so hard that water splashes out of the tub.

"With me, it's like that," says Dad. "Bubbles and bathwater everywhere! Now get into your pajamas. Hurry up! It's dinnertime!"

At dinnertime, Clare's pajamas are inside out and the table is a mess and the mashed potatoes are lumpy.

"Dad," says Clare, "that's not how Mom does it. With Mom, the table is always set just right. And she makes the potatoes extra creamy."

"Ah!" says Dad. "You're not happy with your potatoes? Then maybe it's time for dessert instead."

He pulls out a cupcake with pink frosting and a sugar snowman on top.

"I get dessert without eating dinner?" says Clare.

Dad laughs and says, "With me, it's like that. Dessert instead of dinner. Now eat up and then it's time to get ready for bed."

At bedtime, Dad leaves the light on and reads the story too fast. "Dad," says Clare, "that's not how Mom does it. With Mom, we turn off the big light and turn on the lamp. And she reads slowly so I have time to look at the pictures on every page."

Dad stops reading. He turns off the big light and he switches on the lamp. He even arranges Clare's favorite animals next to her on the pillow.

Then he says, "Okay, let's slow down."

Dad starts the story from the beginning and reads it carefully all the way through.

Then he chooses another.

"This time, we'll do it right."

"Sleep tight, Clare," Dad says.
Clare snuggles into her cozy bed, and as she closes her
eyes she whispers, "Can you be in charge again tomorrow?"

Dad smiles.

First he gives Clare a kiss on the cheek. Then he gives her a light kiss on the nose. Then at last, a BIG kiss on the head, like only Dad does.

Clare sighs happily.

"With me, it's like that," Dad says. "Two bedtime stories and three kisses."

"Now I'll turn off the lamp," says Dad at the end of the book.

"Wait!" says Clare. "I want a kiss like with Mom."